Written and illustrated by Robert Lawson

RABBIT HILL

THE TOUGH WINTER

Written and illustrated by Munro Leaf and Robert Lawson

FERDINAND

WEE GILLIS

THEY WERE STRONG
AND GOOD

THEY WERE STRONG AND GOOD

WRITTEN AND ILLUSTRATED BY

ROBERT LAWSON

THE VIKING PRESS 1940

FOREWORD

This is the story of my mother and my father and of their fathers and mothers.

Most of it I heard as a little boy, so there may be many mistakes; perhaps I have forgotten or mixed up some of the events and people. But that does not really matter, for this is not alone the story of my parents and grandparents, it is the story of the parents and grandparents of most of us who call ourselves Americans.

None of them were great or famous, but they were strong and good. They worked hard and had many children. They all helped to make the United States the great nation that it now is.

Let us be proud of them and guard well the heritage they have left us.

MY MOTHER'S FATHER

MY MOTHER'S FATHER was a Scotch sea captain.

He sailed the brig *Eliza Jane Hopper* from New York to the islands of the Caribbean—to Puerto Rico and Cuba and the Isthmus of Panama.

He used to bring back presents for his friends—monkeys and parrots, sugar cane and sometimes Panama hats.

One time he brought a parrot for one friend and a very fine Panama hat for another. A great storm came on before they reached New York and my mother's father had to stay on deck for two days and two nights.

When the storm was over he went down to his cabin to rest.

The parrot had found the Panama hat and had eaten a great deal of it.

So one friend didn't get his hat, and the other friend *almost* didn't get a parrot.

MY MOTHER'S MOTHER

MY MOTHER'S MOTHER was a little Dutch girl, who lived on a farm in New Jersey.

The City of Paterson stands there now and looks about like this—

But in those days it looked more like this—

The things her father raised on the farm he sold in the city of New York. He used to take them there in a great wagon drawn by four horses.

One time when my mother's mother was quite a big girl he took her along. In the great wagon were hams and corn and cabbages, bacon, beans, salt pork, turnips—and my mother's mother.

They went down to the wharves to sell things to the ships. One of these ships was the *Eliza Jane Hopper* and while the ship's cook was buying salt pork, beans, and turnips for the sailors, my mother's father saw my mother's mother sitting in the great big wagon.

So they were married and went on the *Eliza Jane Hopper* to the islands of the Caribbean for their honey-moon.

My mother's mother liked the monkeys and the sugar cane and the parrots, but she did *not* like sailing on the sea.

My mother's father was tired of the sea too, so they went as far away from it as they could. They went 'way out to Minnesota and lived there. They worked very hard and were strong and good. They had many children and one of them was—

MY MOTHER

WHEN my mother was a little girl there were Indians

in Minnesota. My mother did not like them. They would stalk into the kitchen without knocking and sit on the floor. Then they would rub their stomachs and point to their mouths to show that they were hungry. They would not leave until my mother's mother gave them something to eat.

There were lumberjacks there too. They all came into the town on Saturday nights and made a great deal of noise. And sometimes there were fights.

They frightened my mother.

So my mother's mother sent her to a convent to go to school. It was quiet and peaceful at the convent. The nuns were very gentle and never spoke loudly. My mother liked *them*.

They taught her to paint pictures and to speak French and Spanish and German and Italian, to do beautiful embroidery, and to play the organ. She liked that too.

The nuns had lovely gardens. They taught my mother how to grow flowers and to care for bees. She could open the hives and take out the honey without wearing gloves or a net. Hundreds of bees would light on her hands and face and neck, but none ever stung her. All animals loved my mother because she was so quiet and gentle.

MY FATHER'S FATHER

MY FATHER'S FATHER was an Englishman who lived in Alabama. He was always fighting something. When

he was young he fought the Indians in the Seminole War.
When that was over he decided to be a preacher and fight
the Powers of Evil.

The Government didn't pay him anything while he was
a soldier, but as soon as the war was over it gave him a large
grant of land for having fought the Indians. He already had
all the land he wanted so he traded his grant for a mule. He
used to ride from town to town on his mule and fight with
Satan.

He was a good fighter and had a good loud voice, so people were glad to have him come to their towns and drive out the Powers of Evil.

One time he came to the town where my father's mother lived and fought Satan there.

MY FATHER'S MOTHER

MY FATHER'S MOTHER thought that he had a fine

loud voice and that he fought Satan very well indeed.

So they were married. They worked hard and were strong and good. They had many children and one of them was—

MY FATHER

WHEN my father was very young he had a Negro slave

and two dogs. The dogs were named Sextus Hostilius and Numa Pompilius. The Negro boy was just my father's age and his name was Dick. He and my father and the two hounds used to hunt all day long.

When the Civil War began, my father's father quit fighting Satan and went off to fight the Yankees instead. My father was twelve years old and wanted to go too, but they said he was too young. So he went to work in a store to help out.

The man who owned the store was very wealthy. He had two thousand dollars in gold and a fine pacing horse named Emma G. He wanted to take his money and Emma G. to a safer place, but was afraid to, for the country all about was filled with deserters and runaway slaves.

One evening word arrived that the Yankees were coming. When my father heard that, he said he would ride Emma G. to safety.

They put the gold in a belt under his clothes and all that night he rode through the dark woods. Several times he saw camp fires and twice the next day he was pursued by deserters, but Emma G. could run like the wind and my father was very light, so they got away quite easily.

In the evening of that day, he arrived at the home of the storekeeper's brother in a town far away. They were all glad to see him and gave him five dollars as a reward.

My father was fourteen years old then, so he walked to where the war was and joined General Joseph E. Johnston's army. He was pretty small, so they made him a guidon bearer in the artillery and gave him a mule to ride. It wasn't much of a mule, but my father wasn't much of a man yet, so they got on fine. He named the mule Epaminondas.

The guidon was a small red flag on a long stick. When there was a battle, the Captain would ride out and decide where he wanted the battery placed. My father would sit on his mule at that spot and hold up his flag. Then the cannon would gallop up and form in a line beside the flag, and begin to fire.

My father would sit up very stiff and hold his flag very straight and Epaminondas would stand very still. They were proud to have all the cannon lined up on them.

General Johnston's army had very little food and not nearly as many men as the Yankees, so they always had to retreat. After a while the Captain's horse was killed and the Captain had to take my father's mule. Then my father walked.

There had been four guns in the battery at first, but later there were only three, then two, and finally there was only one. But my father still stood up where the Captain told him to, very stiff and holding his flag very straight. He still felt proud, even though there was only one gun to line up beside him.

Then there was a big battle near Atlanta. When it was over there wasn't even one cannon, or any mule or any Captain, and a Menie ball had hit my father in the leg. He stuck the little red flag under his shirt for a souvenir, used the long stick for a crutch, and went on retreating.

Pretty soon an ammunition wagon picked him up. They had no ammunition left to carry, so they were picking up wounded soldiers. He woke up next day in a hospital. The hospital was a barn and my father was sick there for quite a long time.

By the time my father's leg was well the Yankees had won the war, so he walked back to Alabama. His father had quit fighting Yankees and had gone back to fighting Satan. The store had been burned down and there was no work, and Numa Pompilius and Sextus Hostilius and Dick were all gone too.

My father was sixteen years old then, so he came to New York to make his fortune and went to work in a store there. People used to tease him and call him a little Rebel because of his southern accent.

He didn't make much of a fortune, but he *did* meet my mother. She had come from Minnesota to visit in New York. She didn't laugh at his accent or call him a Rebel, and she felt sorry about the way he limped.

So they were married. They worked hard and were strong and good. They had many children and one of them happened to be ME.

I am proud of my mother and my father and of their mothers and fathers. And I am proud of the country that they helped to build.

THE END